I Have An Autism BOOST!

Jennifer Gilpin Yacio

Illustrated by Lynda Farrington Wilson

I Have An Autism BOOST!

All marketing and publishing rights guaranteed to and reserved by:

FUTURE HORIZONS INC.

Toll-free: 800-489-0727 ~ Fax: 817--277-2270
www.FHautism.com ~ info@FHautism.com
Text © 2021 Jennifer Gilpin Yacio
Illustrations © 2021 Lynda Farrington Wilson
All rights reserved.
Printed in Canada

ISBN: 9781949177763

Introduction by Dr Temple Grandin, author of *The Way I See It*

When I was four, I had no speech and all the signs of autism, such as sensitivity to loud sounds, repetitive behavior, and lack of social interaction. Today, I am a professor of Animal Science at Colorado State University. My mother and many wonderful teachers worked to help me develop my abilities and learn daily living skills such as using manners, shopping, and saving money to buy little toys. Children on the autism spectrum often have uneven skills. They may have abilities and strengths in one area and be good at either art or math. My mother helped me develop my art skills by encouraging me to draw pictures of many different things. If a child is good at math, he/she needs to be advanced to higher level math. One of my autism boosts is visual thinking. This ability has helped me in my career designing for stockyards. It's a boost many people with autism have that can help further their careers, too.

Autism is a very broad spectrum that ranges from Elon Musk at SpaceX and Einstein to more severely challenged individuals who never learn to dress themselves. This book would be ideal for fully verbal, elementary school–aged children may be socially awkward. It emphasizes the positive features of autism, such as attention to detail, special skills, and vast memory. The book can also be used to educate a child's peers about the positive aspects of autism.

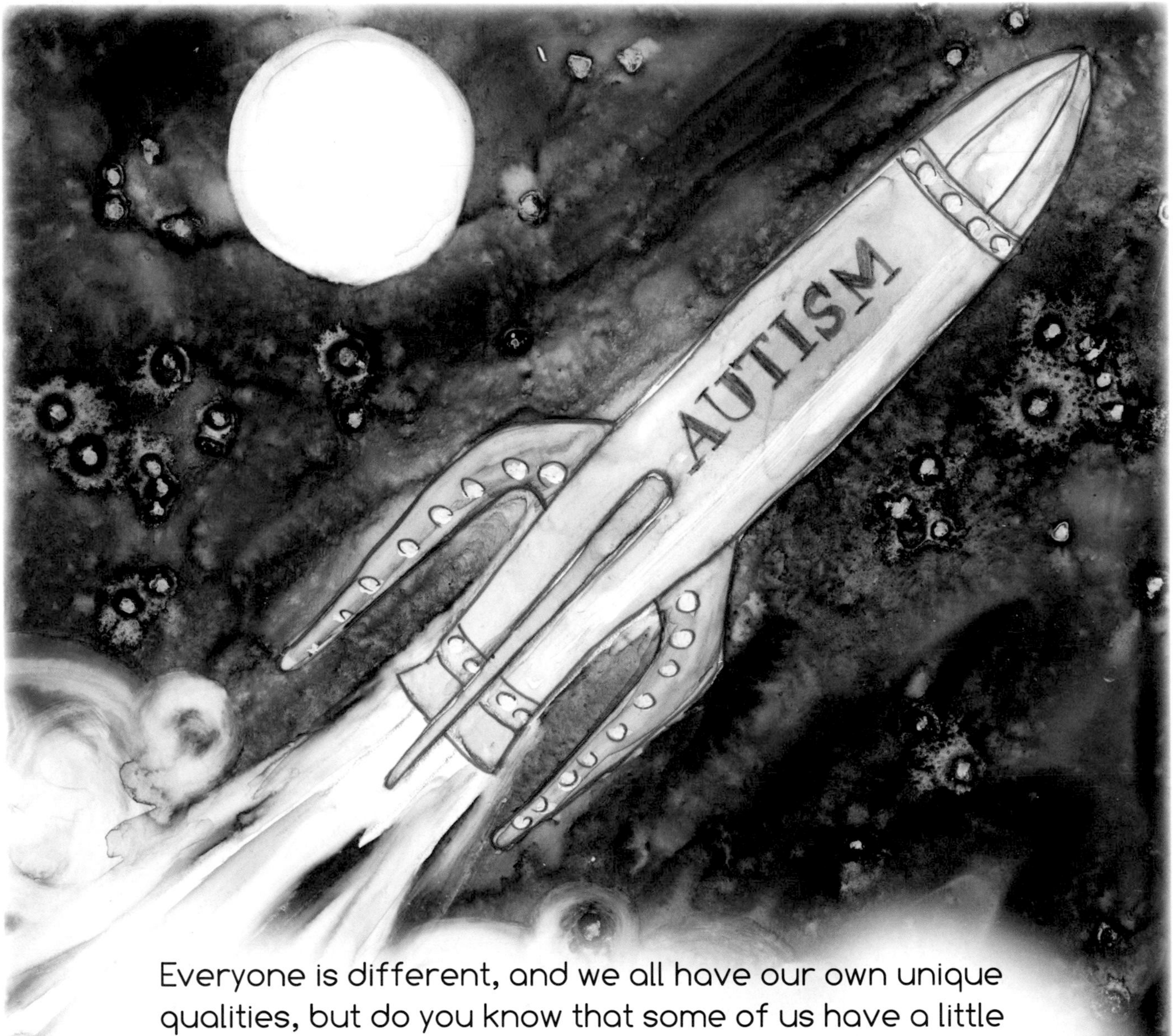

Everyone is different, and we all have our own unique qualities, but do you know that some of us have a little extra—a special BOOST?

It's an autism boost!

1

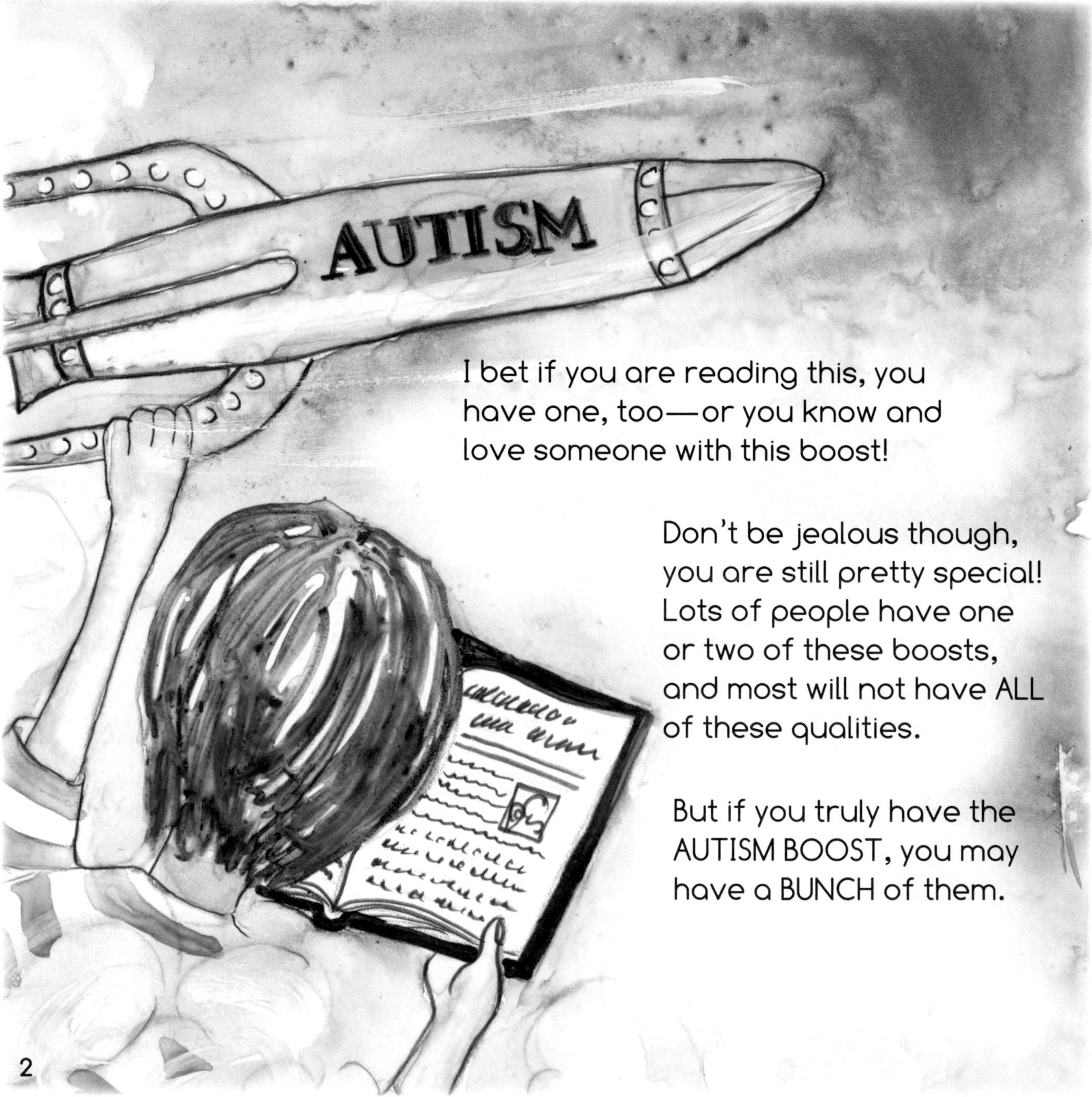

I bet if you are reading this, you have one, too—or you know and love someone with this boost!

Don't be jealous though, you are still pretty special! Lots of people have one or two of these boosts, and most will not have ALL of these qualities.

But if you truly have the AUTISM BOOST, you may have a BUNCH of them.

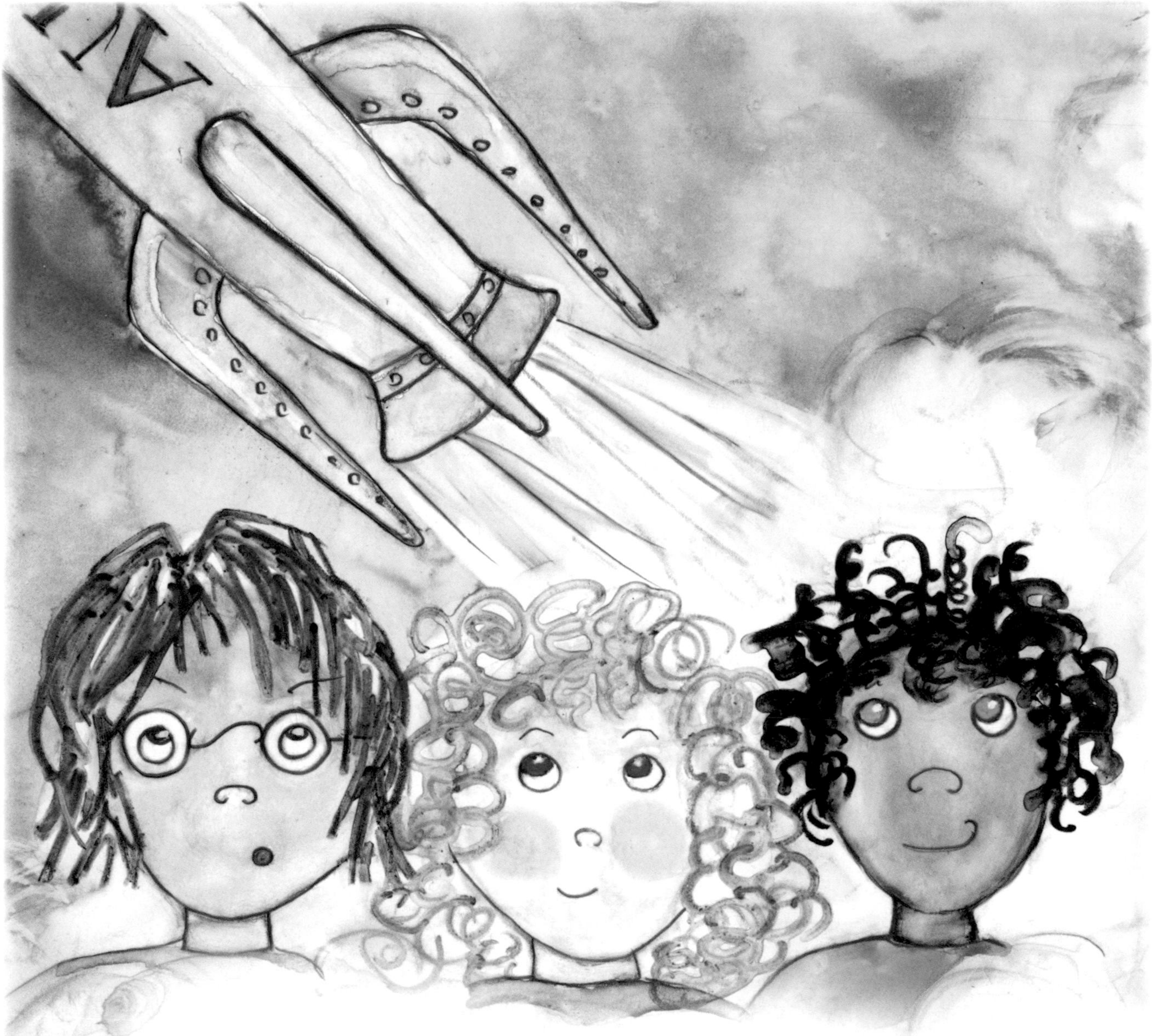

Meet my friends Lucas, Olivia, and Chris as they explain their unique autism boosts!

Hi, I'm Lucas! I can be SUPER focused with great attention to detail. That is just how my brain works, and I don't even have to try!

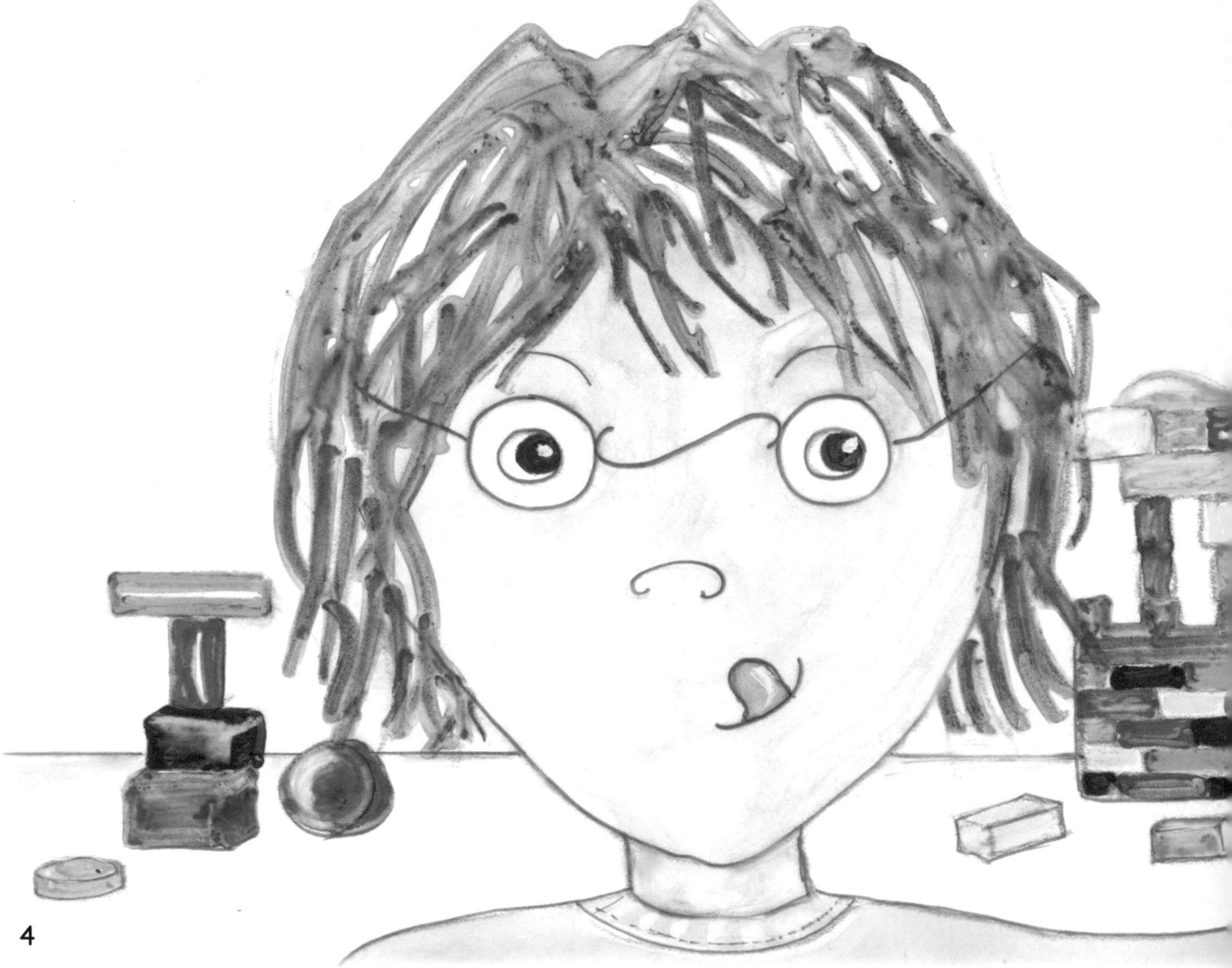

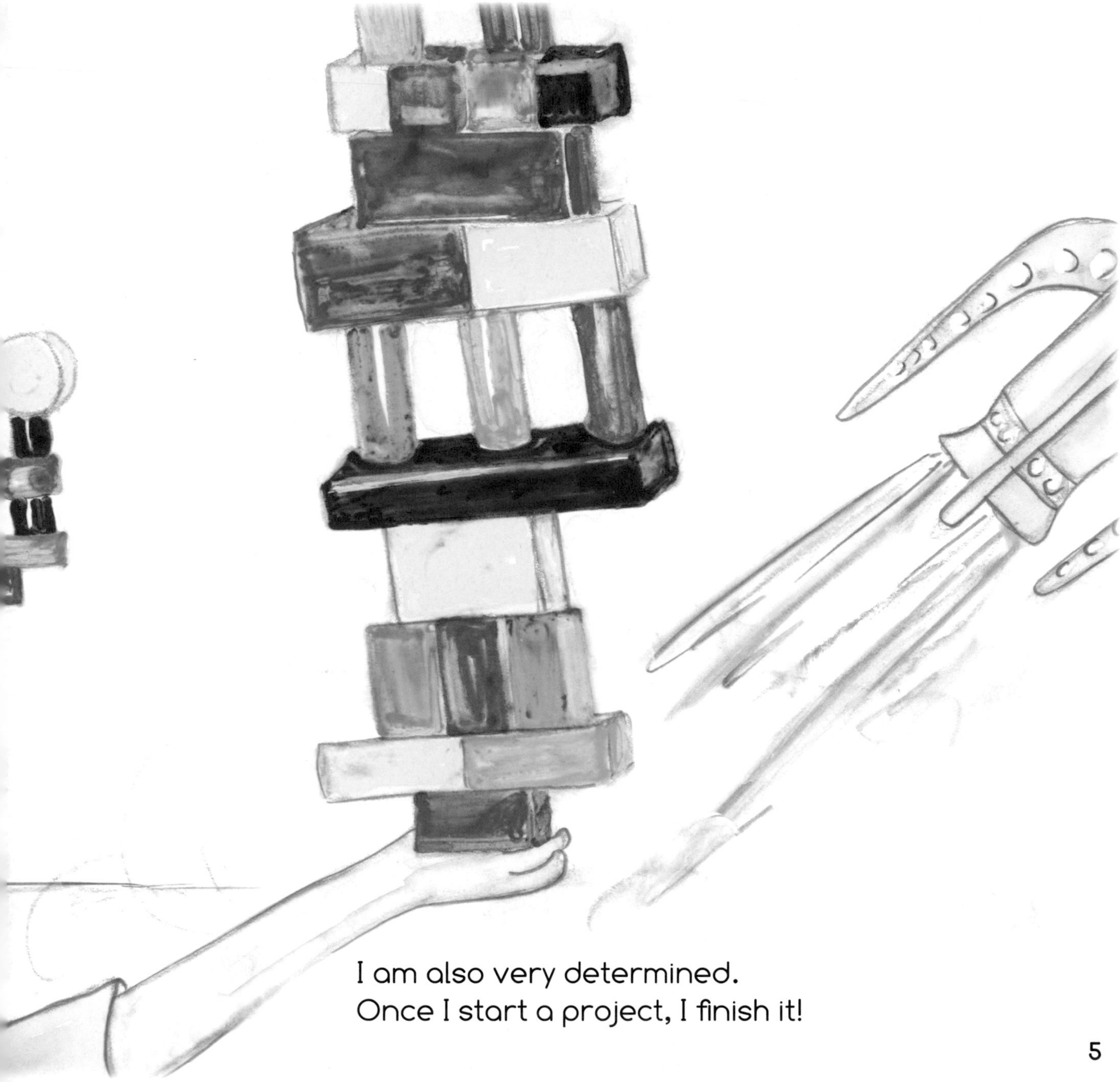

I am also very determined.
Once I start a project, I finish it!

Hi! I'm Olivia. I am very logical. I tend not to use emotions when making important decisions.

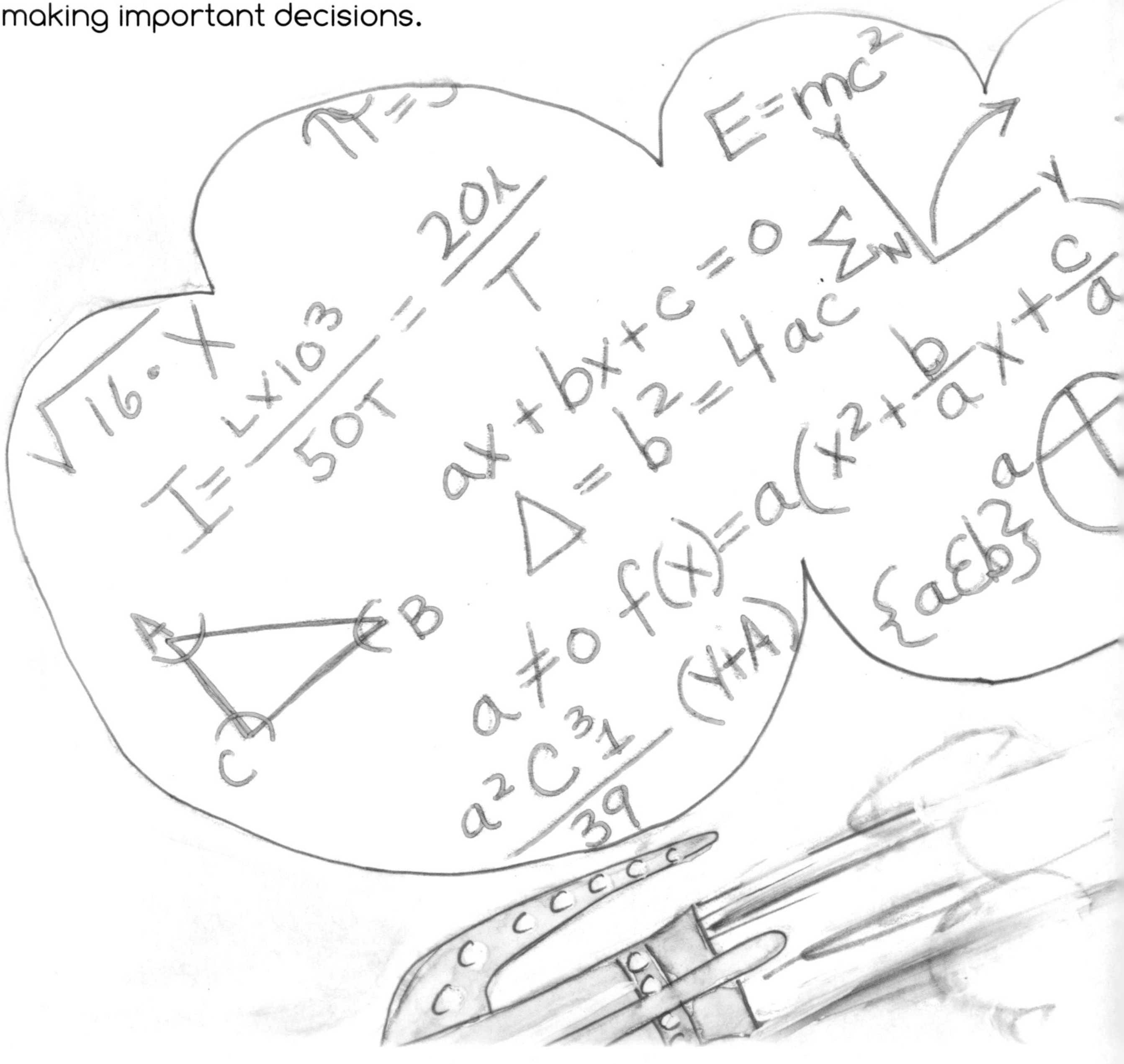

Now, I certainly HAVE emotions—in fact, they are very strong! I am just able to use my head when a problem arises and save my heart 'til later.

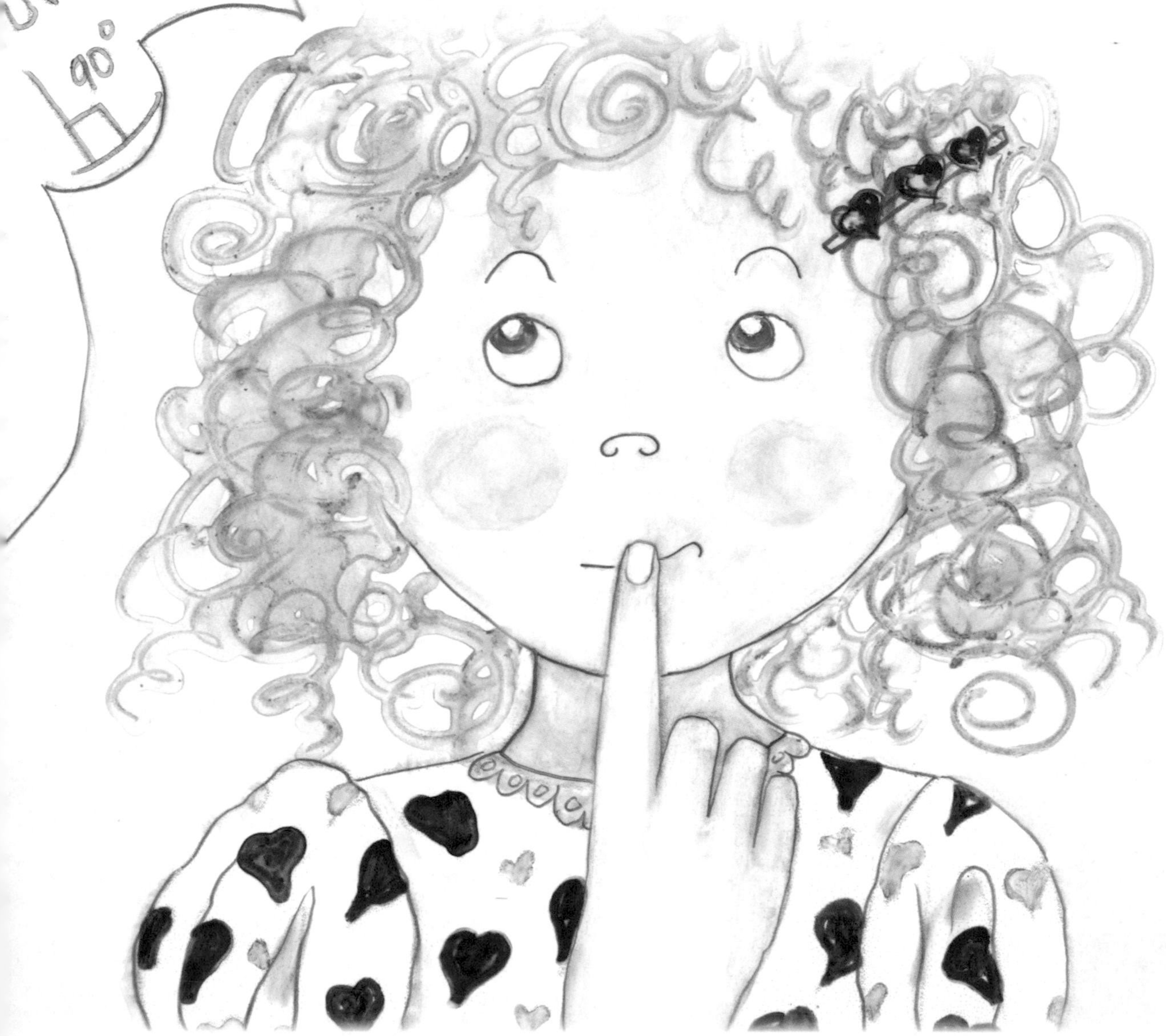

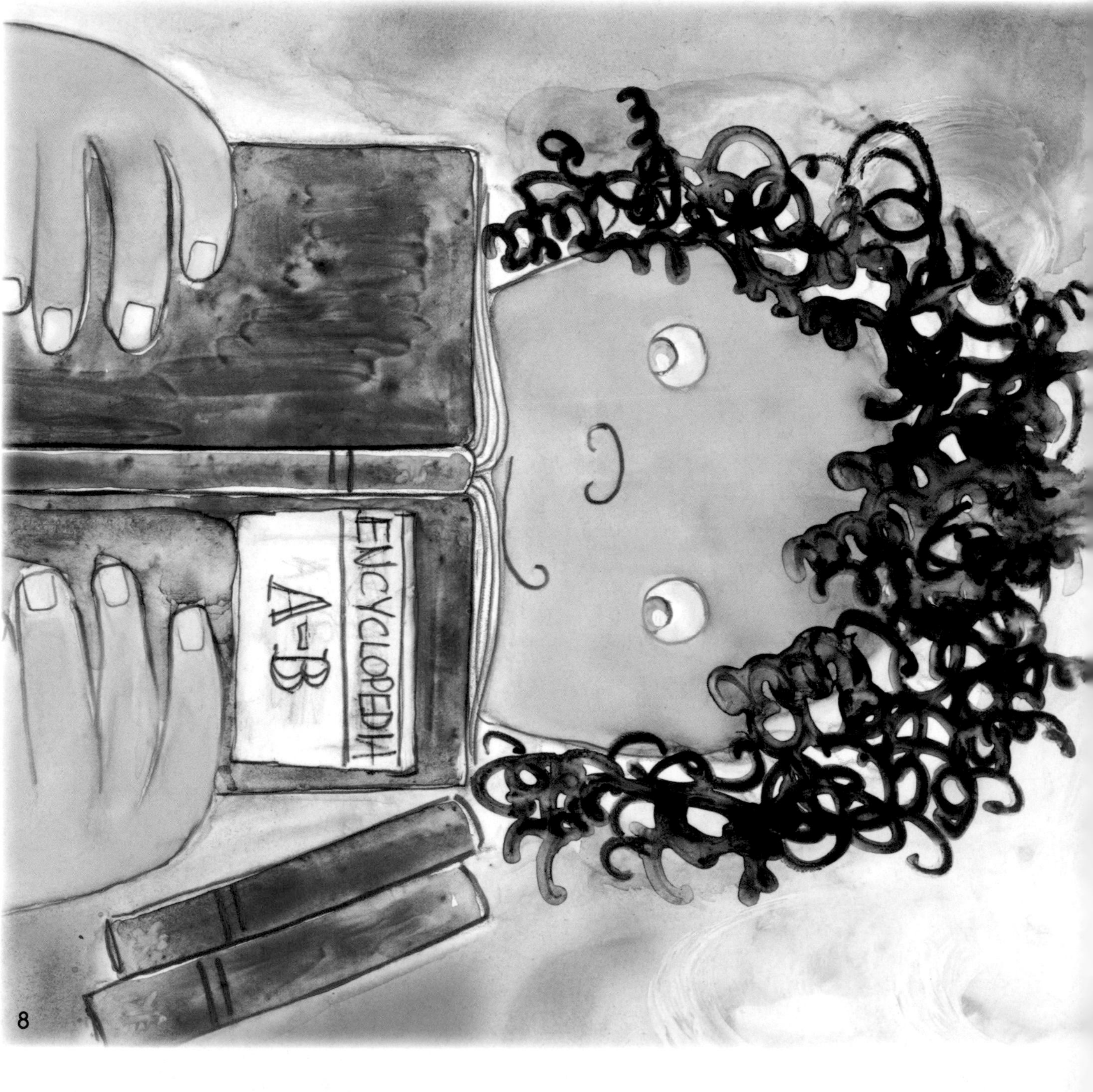

8

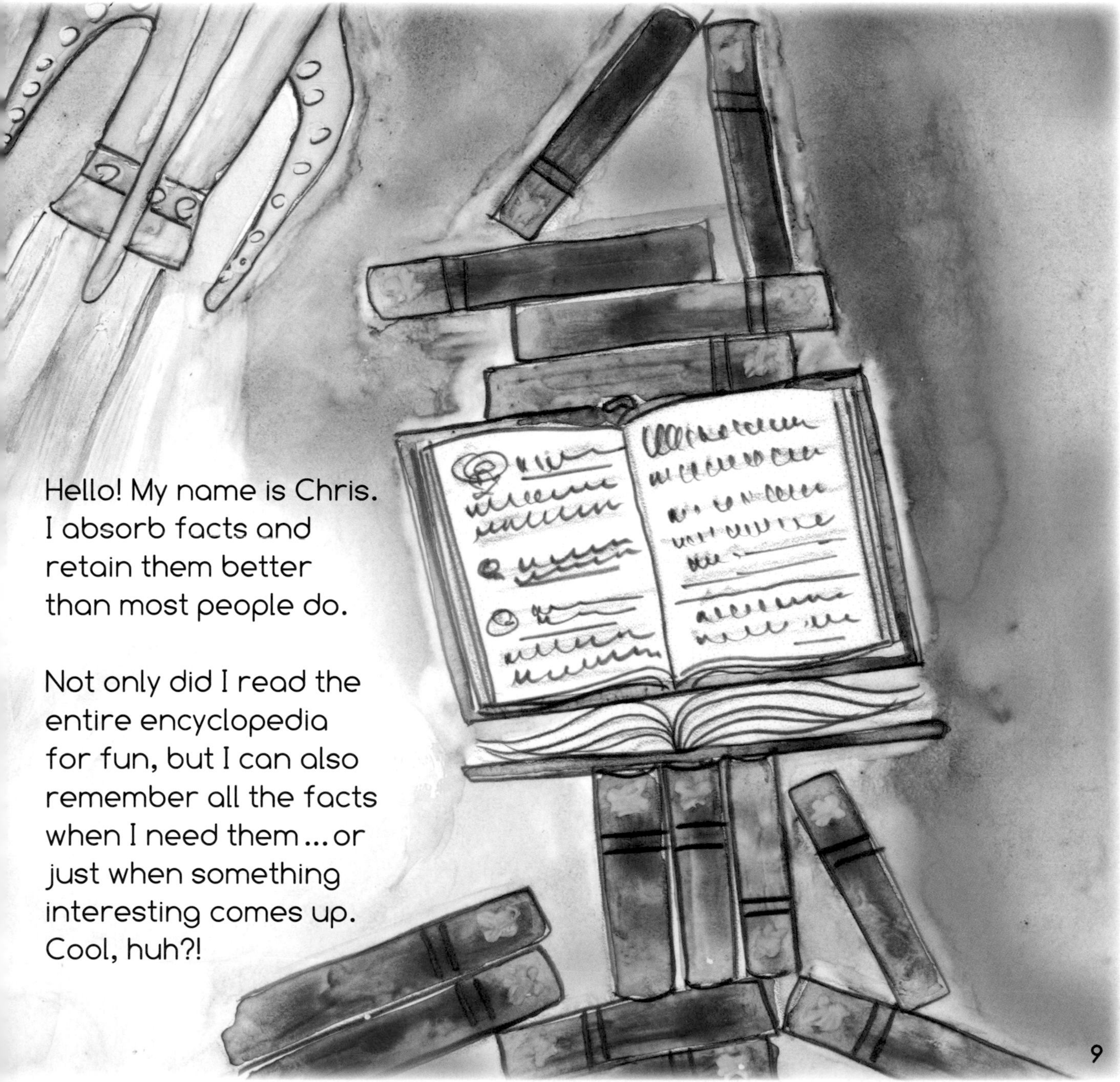

Hello! My name is Chris. I absorb facts and retain them better than most people do.

Not only did I read the entire encyclopedia for fun, but I can also remember all the facts when I need them ... or just when something interesting comes up. Cool, huh?!

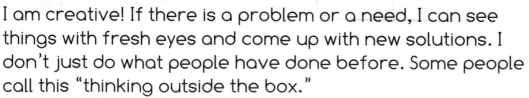

I am creative! If there is a problem or a need, I can see
things with fresh eyes and come up with new solutions. I
don't just do what people have done before. Some people
call this "thinking outside the box."

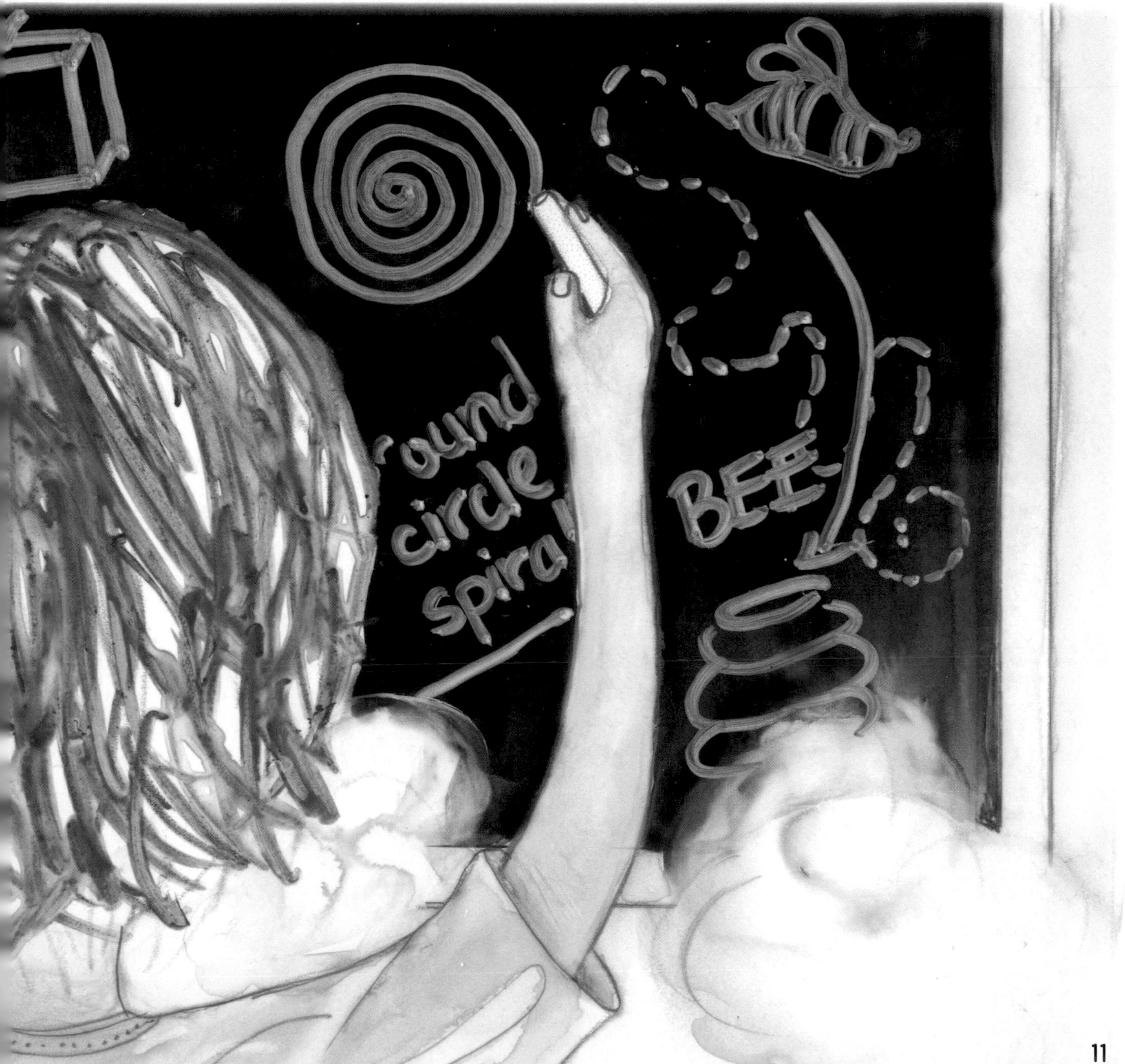

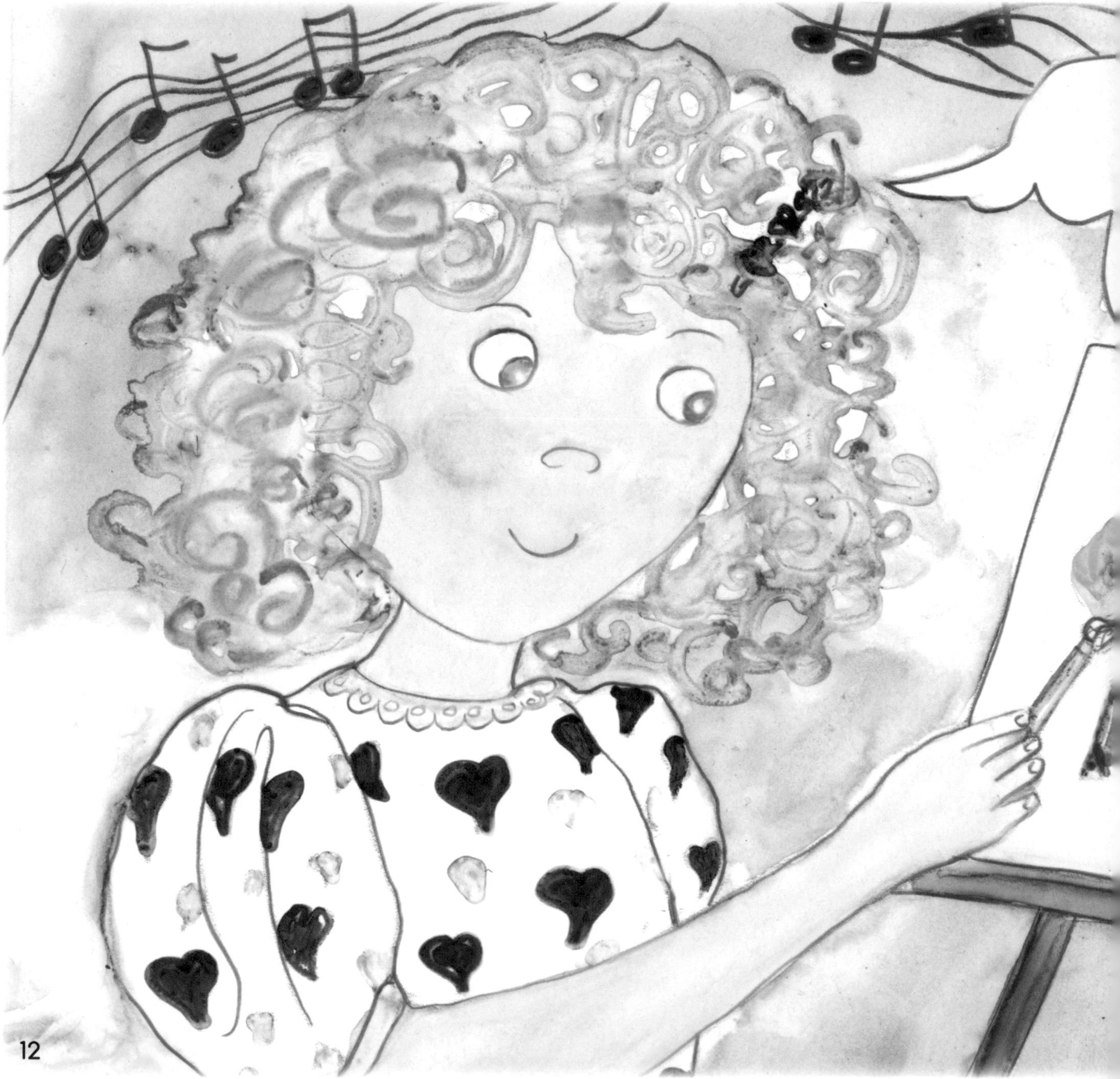

12

I am also creative! I use my creativity in art, theater, and music. I love to express myself this way. Though I do not often show my feelings, I do have so much inside to share.

Painting is my absolute favorite! And with my visual thinking skills, I can see every stroke of a painting in my mind before I even pick up the brush.

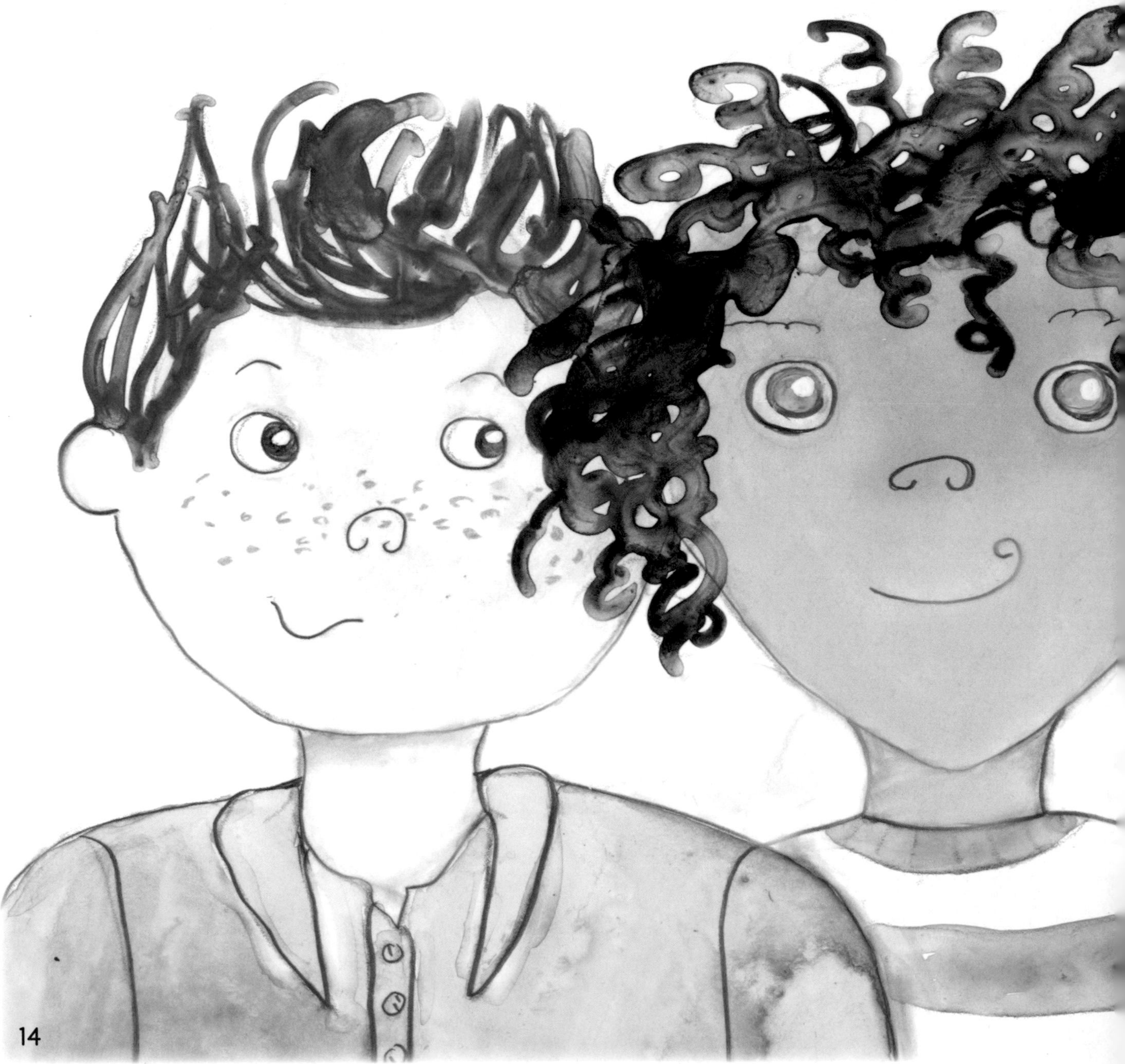

14

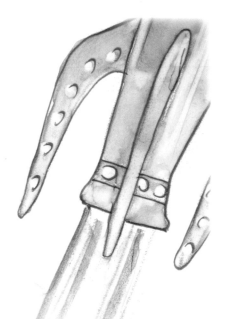

I am a wonderful friend. I've got a lot of integrity. This means I am very honest and loyal, and don't have time for anyone who is not.

With me, what you see is what you get. And you are getting a LOT when you are lucky enough to have me as a friend.

Wow—that's a lot of interesting stuff.
So many cool people have an autism boost.

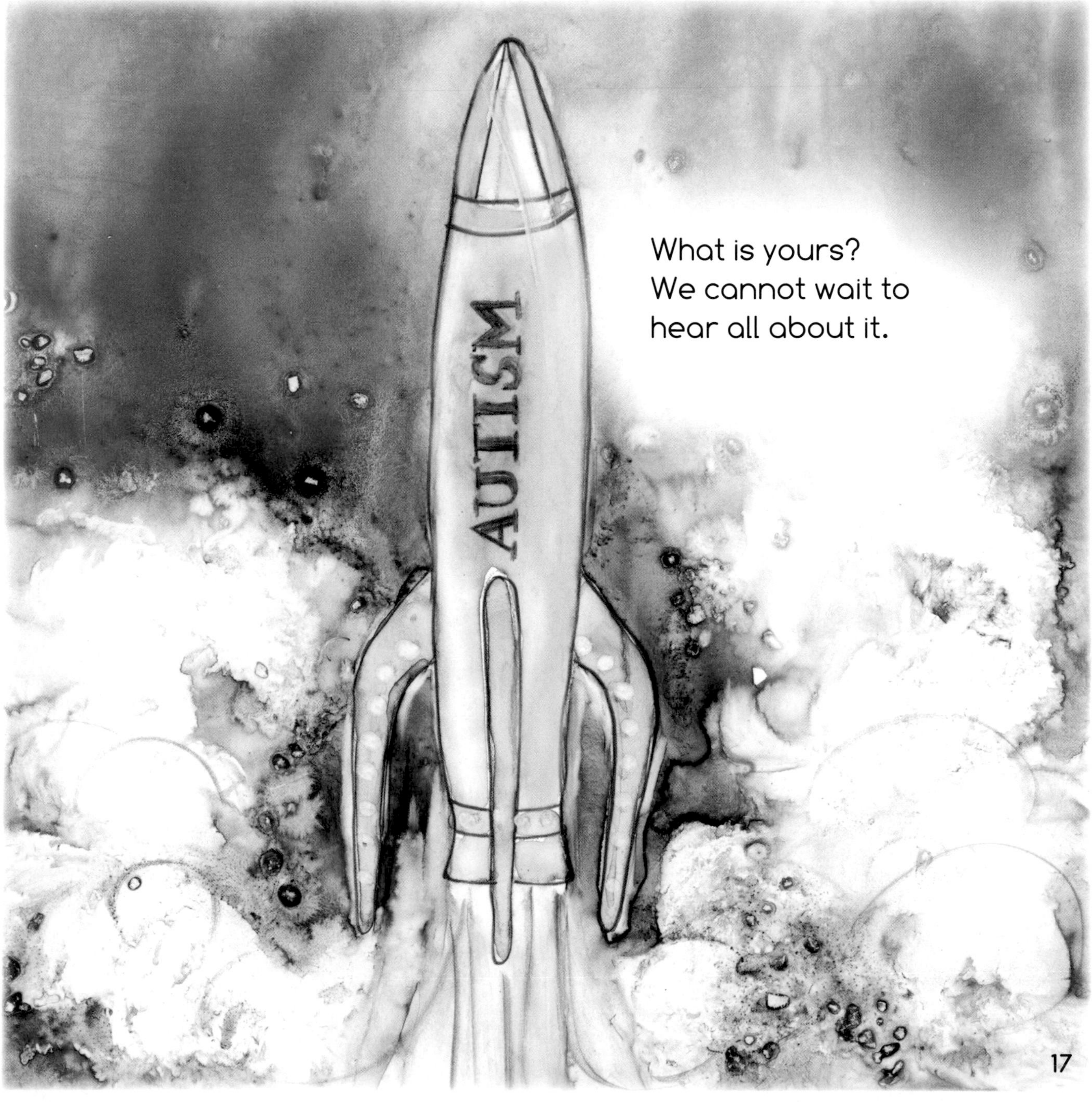

What is yours?
We cannot wait to
hear all about it.

Here is a list of Autism Boosts.

(Circle) or highlight the boosts YOU have.

Ability to learn quickly

Visual thinking

Logical thinking

Great memory

Ability to focus on details

Exceptional honesty

Dependability

Excellent sense of direction

Ability to follow rules well

Ability to concentrate for long periods of time

Problem solving

Creativity

Integrity

Acceptance of differences

Mathematical thinking

Musical ability

What is your biggest or favorite autism boost?

_____

_____

_____

_____

_____

_____

_____

When I grow up, I want to use this boost to:

_____

_____

_____

_____

_____

_____

_____

About the Creators

About the Author

Jennifer Gilpin Yacio is the president of Future Horizons and Sensory World. Ever since her little brother was diagnosed with autism in 1982, she has been interested in autism and how different people perceive the world. With an extensive career in the publishing and autism fields, Jennifer likes to think she also has an autism boost…but that may be wishful thinking.

About the Illustrator

Lynda Farrington Wilson is an artist and former marketing executive. Her talents and experiences have culminated in writing, illustrating, and advocating for children with autism and Sensory Processing Disorder. Lynda and her husband live in North Carolina with their three beautiful sons, the youngest a sensory-seeker with autism. Lynda has illustrated several books and written two children's books: *Squirmy Wormy* and *Autistic? How Silly is That!* You can learn more about her at *www.lyndafarringtonwilson.com*.

DID YOU LIKE THE BOOK?

Rate it and share your opinion.

 **amazon**.com

BARNES&NOBLE
BOOKSELLERS
www.bn.com

Not what you expected? TELL US!

**Most negative reviews occur when the book
did not reach expectations. Did the description
build any expectations that were not met?
Let us know how we can do better.**

Please drop us a line at
info@fhautism.com.
Thank you for your support!

FUTURE HORIZONS INC.

BY THE SAME AUTHOR!

Here is a children's book that will help guide and inspire all kids to reach their full potential. *Temple Did It, and I Can, Too!* explains the obstacles Temple Grandin faced while growing up, then gives the rules she followed to overcome them and become a leading animal scientist.

TEMPLE DID IT, AND I CAN, TOO!

"TIME magazine Person of the Year"

"she couldn't talk"

"doesn't look at me"

"Why is she screaming?"

"world renowned scientist"

A CHILD'S GUIDE TO REACHING LIFE GOALS

Introduction by Dr. Temple Grandin

by Jennifer Gilpin Yacio

Illustrated by Lynda Farrington Wilson

Introduction written by *Dr Temple Grandin*, herself!